This igloo book belongs to:

....

Published in 2013
by Igloo Books Ltd
Cottage Farm
Sywell
NN6 0BJ
www.igloobooks.com

SHE001 1113
2 4 6 8 10 9 7 5 3
ISBN: 978-1-78197-527-5

Printed and manufactured in China

Illustrated by
Mike Garton, Jacqueline East and
Kay Widdowson

My First Story Book

igloobooks

Contents

Stories

for **1**
Year
Olds

The Bell on the Bus

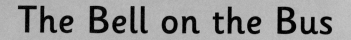

Ring-a-ding-ding, goes the bell on the bus.
"Put out your hand, it'll stop for us."

Suzy, Jonny, Derek and Dot,
get on the bus at the green bus stop.

Ring-a-ding-ding, everyone holds on tight.
The little bus swings to the left, then the right.

The red bus stops for Milly and Pete.
They pay their fares and find a seat.

Up the steep hill, the little, red bus rumbles.
Brrm-brrm-chug, the engine grumbles.

Chug-chug-brrm, it's nearly at the top.
Walter's waiting at the blue bus stop.

Ring-a-ding-ding, it's a bit of a squash.
Down in the town, everybody gets off.

14

The little red bus goes, *vroom, vroom, vroom.*
Ring-a-ding-ding, it'll be back again soon.

15

Bath Time for Bo

One lovely, sunny morning, Bo was curled up in her bed.
Mommy came into her room. "Wake up," she said.

Mommy gave Bo a cuddle and said, "It's time for your morning wash. We'll make the water nice and warm, then we'll *splish and splosh.*"

Mommy got a big, bath towel and Bo's special fairy mat. "Let's put some water in the bath," she said. Then, Mommy turned on the faucets.

Swoosh, went the bath water into the bath. It swirled and went, *drip-drop*. Then, Mommy turned the bath faucets off and the water stopped, *plip-plop*.

"There now, baby Bo," said Mommy and she held Bo in the bath. She scooped some water on her back and it tickled and made Bo laugh.

Mommy got the dolphin soap. She rubbed it on Bo's tummy.
She pulled lots of silly faces. Bo thought Mommy was funny.

Mommy got the big, bath towel and rubbed Bo's little toes.
She dressed her in a babygro and wiped the
bubbles off her nose.

Then, Mommy picked up Rubber Duck and patted him dry, too. "Look," said Mommy to baby Bo, "he's had bath time, just like you."

Playtime Fun

Jenny is coming to Ben's house today.
Ding-dong, goes the doorbell. It's time to play.

Open up the toy box. Pull out all the toys.
There are beeps, squeaks and rattles. What a lot of noise!

Here's a yellow digger, its engine goes, *brrm, brrm*.
Red racing car is very fast, it whizzes off — *vroom, vroom*.

Boing, boing, goes the little, blue ball, bouncing up and down.
Choo-choo, goes the little train, chuffing round and round.

The red bus goes, *ding-ding*. The telephone goes *ring-ring-ring*.
Toot, goes the car and *bang*, goes the drum.
Making noise is lots of fun.

Tick, tock, goes the clock on the playroom wall. *Ding-dong,* goes the doorbell in the hall. Jenny's mommy has come to call.

It's time to put the toys away.
"Never mind," says Mom. "You can play another day."

Jenny waves and says, "Goodbye, Ben.
I'm glad you're my best playtime friend."

31

The Little, Blue Train

Everyone is patiently waiting on the platform of the station.
The little, blue train comes, *choo, choo, choo*.
It huffs and puffs and goes, *whoo-whoo-whoo*.

"All aboard!" cries the station master.
Soon, the train will be moving faster.

Clunk, go the doors and *click,* go the locks. The whistle blows and the train pulls off, rolling, rolling down the track. The little, blue train's wheels go, *clickety-clack, clickety-clack.*

Past the fields and the cows and the sheep. Up the hill that's very steep. Slowly, slowly, *chuff-chuff-chuff*. The little, blue train goes, *puff-puff-puff*.

Then it's down the other side, *whoo-whoo-whoo*.
The little, blue train is rolling, *choo-choo-choo*.
Through the tunnel, where it's all black,
clickety-clack, clickety-clack, clickety-clack.

"Look," says the driver, "we're nearly there."
The little, blue train puffs clouds into the air.
Then it slows, *click-clack,* on the railway track.

Slowly, slowly it comes to a stop.
"It's the end of the line," says the driver. "Everybody off."

It's been a long day for the little, blue train.
After a nice long sleep, it'll be back again.
Goodnight, little, blue train.

Bedtime Frogs

It was nearly bedtime in the little frogs' house. "Hop upstairs," said Mother Frog, "and brush your teeth. Then, put on your pajamas, it's time to go to sleep."

41

One little frog gave a big, dry croak.
He cried and said, "I've got a sore throat."

"I've got a sore throat, too," croaked another.
Soon, all the little frogs were croaking at their mother.

"Hush, now," said Mother Frog. "Wait there,
I'll be back soon." Then, she opened up a cupboard
and got some medicine and a spoon.

44

Mother Frog's medicine was drippy, gloopy and runny.
A spoonful each for the frogs slid right down to their tummies.

Soon, all the little frogs were tucked up in their beds.
Mother read them a story and kissed their little heads.

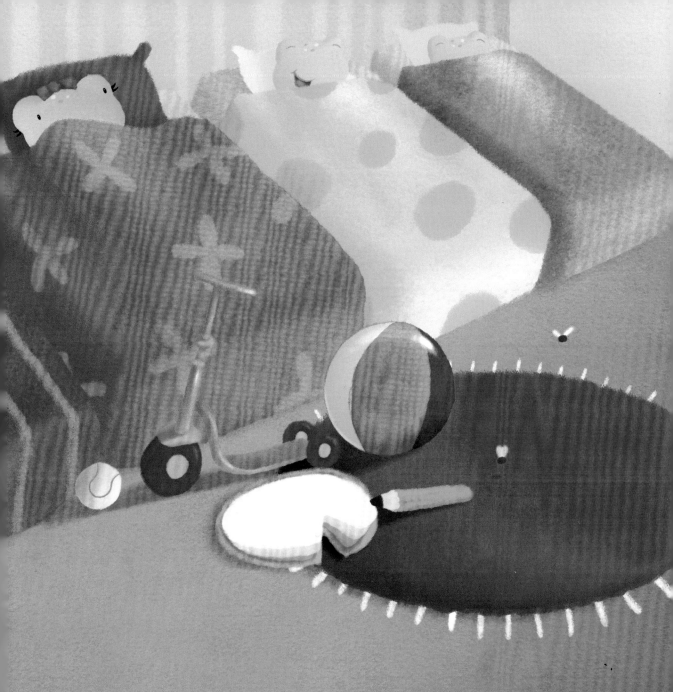

No one made a sound, as Mother turned out the light.
All the frogs were very sleepy. "Goodnight, little frogs,"
said Mother, "goodnight."

Where's the Moon?

Lionel looked out of the window one night.
There were no stars or bright moonlight.

"Where are the stars?" he asked, "Where's the moon?
Are they gone forever? Will they come back soon?"

"They're busy putting the sun to bed.
You can call to them," Mommy said.

"All you have to say is, *come out stars, come out moon, shine your light in my bedroom.*"

51

So, Lionel called to the moon and the stars. Then, all that
night he had sweet dreams, sleeping under
starlight and soft moonbeams.

Stories for 2 Year Olds

Amy's Game

Daddy said to Amy, "Let's play hide-and-seek. I'll count from one to ten. I promise I won't peek. 1-2-3-4-5-6-7-8-9-10."

Then, Daddy crept across the carpet and looked behind
the door. He peered into the closet and all around the floor.
"Where are you, Amy?" he asked.

Dad opened up the lid of Amy's green toy box. Then, he looked inside the jumper drawer and the drawer stuffed full of socks.

"Where could she be?" said Dad. Then he looked under the bed.
"Amy isn't here, either," and then he scratched his head.

He went into the hallway and peered down the stairs.
"Amy's good at hiding," said Dad. "I can't find her anywhere."

Then, someone gave a chuckle. They shuffled and they wriggled.
From underneath the pink bedspread, there came a little giggle.

So, Dad crept across the carpet. He peeped and said, "BOO!"
Amy jumped up squealing and Dad said, "I found you!"

"It's my turn to hide," said Dad. "Remember now, don't peek."
So, Amy counted from one to ten. She loved playing
hide-and-seek.

Fiona's Post

Fiona didn't like it when the postman came to call.
He lurked behind the letterbox and dropped letters in the hall.

He made the garden gate go creak and shut it with a *thwack*. Then, he crunched along the gravel path, carrying his letter sack.

One very special morning, the delivery was late.
Then, suddenly, Fiona heard the creaking of the gate.

The postman rang the bell and Fiona ran to hide.
She crept under the stairs, in case Mom let him inside.

Fiona peeped out at the postman. He was big and very tall.
He handed Mom a parcel and she put it by the wall.

The postman said the parcel had come from far away.
"It's for you, Fiona," he said, "because today is your birthday."

In the parcel was a lovely teddy, from Fiona's Auntie Sue.
The postman delivered it especially. Fiona said, "Thank you."

Fiona was very glad the postman had come to call. She waved and gave him a great, big smile — he wasn't frightening at all.

Billy and Cuddles

Billy and Cuddles loved the rain. They watched it drip-drop down the window pane. "Can we go outside and splash about?" Billy asked.

"Yes," said Mom. "Both of you must put on your wellies and your raincoats. Remember now, don't get too muddy or wet."

Outside, Cuddles saw a puddle and she jumped in the middle.
The water splashed Billy and it made Cuddles giggle.

So, Billy gave a jump and splashed in a puddle.
It was very muddy and splattered Cuddles.
"My turn," said Cuddles with a chuckle and she
looked for another puddle.

The puddle was deep and the water began to creep down Cuddles' boots and between her toes. "It's cold!" she cried.

Cuddles jiggled her boots, this way and that.
She jiggled too much and whoops, she slipped — *splat*,
into the very muddy puddle.

"I'm wet," said Billy. "So are you, Cuddles.
I've had enough of jumping in puddles."
So, they went back home to play inside.

Mom gave them cupcakes and fizzy lemonade.
"We still love the rain," said Billy and Cuddles,
"especially jumping in puddles."

The Lost Yellow Ball

Ned and Lola had lost their big, yellow ball. So, they sniffed all over the house. Then, they sniffed in the garden.

There was something round on the ground, in the
vegetable patch. "It's our ball!" said Ned, but when he sniffed it,
he cried, "Pooh! It's just a smelly, old cabbage."

"I'll look in the shed," said Lola and she sniffed and sniffed.
The shed was dark and full of spiders hanging in cobwebs.

Sniff, sniff went Lola. Then, a big spider ran onto her nose. "Urgh!" she cried, jumping and bumping into Dad's garden tools. They clanged and clattered with a terrible noise.

Lola bounded out of the shed and across the lawn. Then, with one big leap, she jumped over the wall. There was something squashy and soft on the other side.

"It's our big, yellow ball," said Ned.
"Well done, Lola, you found it after all."

All afternoon, Ned and Lola had fun with their ball. It went *boing* on the shed and *bounce-bounce* on the wall.

They ran around and giggled, then ran around some more.
Ned and Lola were happy. They loved their big, yellow ball.

Tomboy Tina

Tina's mom was having a party. "Cousin Zara is coming early to play," she said. "Do you want to put on a dress and some shoes?"

Tina just shook her head. "I don't want a dress, or shoes,"
she said. "I want to wear my scruffy dungarees,
so I can climb up trees."

Then, Cousin Zara arrived. She sparkled like stars, all glitter and spangles. She wore a fancy hairband and red, jingly bangles.

Zara twirled on her tiptoes and it seemed to Tina that she was just like a fairy, or a ballerina.

Tina thought Zara was terribly clever. "I want to be just like you," she said. "You're the best cousin, ever."
"Shall I show you how?" asked Zara.

"You don't have to wear shoes or a dress." That made
Tina smile. She nodded and said, "Yes!"

Zara helped Tina to pick out some clothes. She gave her bracelets and hairbands and put pink polish on her toes.

Soon, Tina was ready for the party. Mom gave her a squeeze.
"You look beautiful, Tina," she said, "even in dungarees."

Bedtime for Ted

It was night-time in Edward's house. He wouldn't go to bed. "I'm not going," he said to Dad, "not without Big Ted."

Dad and Edward looked high and low and searched from here to there. They simply couldn't spot Big Ted hiding anywhere.

Then, Dad said, "Look, I can see a furry head. I've found your teddy, Edward — he's already in the bed."

"Naughty Big Ted," said Edward, but he gave him a cuddle.
At bedtime there's nothing like a teddy bear to snuggle.

"Goodnight, Edward," said Dad. "Goodnight, Teddy."
There was no reply because they were asleep already.

Stories
for 3
Year
Olds

Carrie the Climber

Carrie's brother, Ben, had climbed up to the tree house in their garden. "I want to climb up, too," said Carrie. Ben pulled up the ladder and said, "No, Carrie, you can't come up."

"You're too small to climb the ladder," said Dad.
"It's a little bit too high," said Mom.
Carrie was determined to climb up to the tree house.

So, when no one was looking, Carrie went to the shed and pulled out her play chair and her plastic toy box. "I'll be big enough to climb up, now," she said.

Carrie climbed onto the box and then onto the chair. "I'm nearly there," she said and she gave a little kick. The chair slipped and fell with a *thunk*, onto the grass. "Help!" cried Carrie. "I'm stuck!"

Ben looked down and Mom looked up. Then, Dad ran
as fast as he could to the bottom of the tree. He reached up to
Carrie and said, "Hold on to me." Soon, Carrie
was safe and sound, back on the ground.

"It is important to listen to what we say," said Mom.
"I'm going to be a tree climber," said Carrie.
Everyone smiled. "We know you will," they said.

Bonny's Dolly

Bonny had lost her best dolly on holiday. When she came home, she played with Teddy and she played with Bunny, but it wasn't the same. "I want my best dolly!" cried Bonny.

Mom gave Bonny a lovely, soft cuddle. "Would you like to go next door and play with Cilla?" she asked.
"That will cheer you up."
"Yes, please," said Bonny and she wiped away her tears.

At Cilla's house, Bonny did a drawing and played on the swing.
Then, Cilla's mom brought out the toy box. It was full of toys.

"Look, here's my best dolly," said Cilla with a great, big smile. Poor Bonny didn't have a best dolly to play with anymore and she began to cry.

"Don't worry, Bonny," said Cilla's mommy, gently. "There are lots of pretty dollies here to play with." She got them out of the toy box. "Pick the one you like the most," she said.

Bonny had a lovely time playing with the dollies. Cilla and her mommy were very kind because they let Bonny keep the one she liked the best. "Thank you," said Bonny. She was very happy. It felt lovely to have a new best dolly.

Well Done, Leonard

A stranger had come to live at Leonard's house. Mom said it was Leonard's baby brother and he was called Charlie. Dad said that Leonard was a big brother now and it was a very important job, but Leonard didn't like being a big brother.

Charlie couldn't talk, or run about, or play in the garden.
In fact, he spent most of the time asleep. "Being a big
brother is boring," said Leonard.

One day, Mom was busy cleaning. The vacuum cleaner whirred and crackled and made a terrible racket. Charlie woke up and began to cry. Mom couldn't hear and Dad couldn't hear, but Leonard could hear.

He ran into the living room and tugged at Mom's arm.
"Charlie's crying," he said. So, Mom went to give Charlie
a cuddle. "Well done, Leonard," she said.
"Well done," said Dad. "You're a very good, big brother."

As a special treat, Mom and Dad took Leonard to the park.
He slid down the slide and whirled around on the roundabout.

"I can't wait for Charlie to be old enough to play with,"
said Leonard. "Being a big brother is the best thing ever."

Bubbles Learns to Swim

Bubbles wanted to swim with his friends, but every time he tried, he just kept sinking and blowing big, watery bubbles. "I don't like swimming," he said, splashing about in his spotty armbands.

"Swish your arms and kick your legs, like me," said Dad.
When Bubbles tried, water shot up his nose and into his ears.
"I hate swimming," he spluttered.

Everyone else had a lovely time swimming in the pool. Alex and Sammy were whizzing down the waterslide. "Come on, Bubbles," they said. "It's great fun."

Bubbles felt very cross. "Swimming is rubbish," he shouted, kicking his legs and swishing his arms, angrily. Then, suddenly, Bubbles began to move.

"Bubbles, you're swimming!" cried Dad. "Keep going."
Soon, Bubbles was able to swim right across to his friends.
"Well done, Bubbles!" they cried.

It wasn't long before Bubbles was having fun on the waterslide, too. "Yippee!" he cried, as he went, SPLASH! into the water. "I love swimming."

The Shiny, Red Shoes

Angelina was very excited. She was going to a party at Pippa the hippo's house. "Do you want to wear your shiny, red shoes?" asked Mom. "They'll match your dress."

"No, thank you," said Angelina. "I'm going to wear my blue shoes."

"You wear your blue shoes every day," said Mom. "The red ones will look much nicer."
"No, thank you," said Angelina.

At Pippa the hippo's house, Angelina waved to her friend, Sarah. She had a lovely, yellow party dress on and shiny shoes to match. Angelina looked down at her everyday, blue shoes and she realized they looked very scruffy.

Then, Tommy came running over to say hello. He had his best jeans on and lovely, new trainers. Angelina looked down at her blue shoes. They didn't look very nice at all.

"I wish I'd worn my shiny, red shoes," said Angelina and her lip quivered. Mom gave a big smile and pulled Angelina's shiny, red shoes out of her handbag. "I brought them along, just in case you changed your mind," she said.

Angelina was very happy. She quickly put on the shiny, red shoes. "Thank you, Mommy," she said. "I love you almost as much as my lovely, red shoes." Then, Angelina ran inside and had a lovely time at Pippa the hippo's party.

Don't Worry, Wanda

Wanda was on the roundabout at the park. Round and round, it whizzed and swished. Wanda was worried that it would go too fast.

"I feel dizzy," she wailed, "I want to get off."
"Don't worry, Wanda," said Mom. "We'll try the swings instead."

The swing swung back and forth. Wanda was worried that it would go too high. Her little chin quivered and she began to cry.

"My tummy feels funny and I want to get off," she sobbed.
"Don't worry, Wanda," said Mom and she took her hand.
"We'll try the slide instead."

At the slide, Mom said, "I'll hold your hand. Let's count to three."
So, Mom counted one, two, three and *wheee!* Wanda slid all the
way to the bottom.

"That was fun!" cried Wanda. "Can I do it again?"
Very soon, Wanda was sliding down all by herself and Mom was
very pleased. "You see, Wanda," she said, "there's really
no need to worry at all."

Franky's Shadow

One night, Franky had a bad dream. So, he got out of bed and crept along the landing to Mom and Dad's room. Something was following Franky.

It was big and gray and had arms and legs. When Franky moved, it moved, too. When Franky stood still, it also stood still. Franky didn't like the strange shape following him.

"MOMMY!" cried Franky, at the top of his voice. "There's a monster following me." Mom and Dad came running out of their room. "It's not a monster," said Mom. "It's your shadow."

"My shadow had a bad dream, too," said Franky.
So, Mom and Dad took Franky to snuggle down in
their room. After that, there were no more bad
dreams for Franky, or his shadow.

Night, Night, Fred

It was time for bed at Fred's house. "Come on, Fred," said Dad. "The sun's asleep and the moon is bright. It's time to put away your toys and say goodnight."

Fred didn't want to go to bed. He wanted to play with his toys. "No," he said. "Come on, now," said Dad and he held out his arms. Fred took two steps back and he shook his head and his cheeks went red. "No bed," he said.

"Well," sighed Dad. "Let's play a game instead. Let's pretend the toys are tired after the day. They can't go to sleep until they're put away. Could you help me to tuck them up in the toy box and say goodnight?" Fred looked at his toys and he looked at Dad. Then he thought for a while and said, "Alright."

Fred picked up his toys and he kissed them goodnight.
Dad closed the lid of the toy box tight. Fred gave a sigh and he
rubbed his eyes. "I'm tired," he said. "Come on," whispered
Dad and he gently picked up Fred and laid him in his bed.

Fred snuggled into his warm, snoozy quilt and his soft pillow. Dad was very proud. "Well done," he said, "goodnight," and he turned out the light. Outside, the moon shone bright, but Fred didn't see because he was fast asleep. Night, night, Fred.

Stories
for 4
Year
Olds

Walter to the Rescue

Walter the giraffe was playing at the park
with his friends, but he wasn't very happy.
"What's the matter, Walter?" asked Josh.
"You're all having loads of fun," said Walter. "I'm too
big for the climbing frame. I'm not having any fun at all."

"Why don't you have a go on the slide?" said Sammy.
When Walter got onto the slide, his long legs nearly reached the
bottom. "You see?" said Walter, feeling very annoyed.
"I am just too tall to have fun."

"Let's play chase," said Josh. Walter's friends were very quick and whizzed round and round. Walter couldn't turn his long legs that quickly and he soon got caught. "It's no fun being me," he said, hanging his head.

Suddenly, there was a loud cry. "Help, help!" said a voice. "I'm stuck!" It was Walter's friend, Elly. She had climbed right up to the top of the climbing frame, but now she was too frightened to climb back down.

Walter quickly went over on his long, graceful legs. "Don't worry Elly," he said. "Climb onto my neck and I'll lower you down." So, Elly climbed onto Walter's neck and she was soon safely on the ground. Everyone cheered and said, "Hooray for Walter!"

"Thank you for rescuing me, Walter," said Elly.
"It's a good job you've got long legs and a long neck."
Walter felt shy and he went a bit red. "Maybe it's
not so bad being me after all," he said.

Charlie's Big Dig

One day, Charlie invited his friend, Roly, round to play.
"Make sure you don't get up to any mischief," said Mom.
"We won't," said Charlie and Roly, as they ran off outside to
see what interesting things they could find to do.
"I wish we had some swings, or a slide to play on," said Charlie.

Just then, there was the sound of
shuffling and giggling coming from next door.
"You go first," said a voice. "No, you go first," said another.
Suddenly, a small furry head bounced right up above the fence.

A few minutes later, another furry head bounced up and down.
Charlie and Roly tried to jump up, to see who it was, but
the fence was too high. No matter how hard they tried, they
couldn't jump high enough to see over it.

"I want to find out who's bouncing next door," said Charlie. "Me, too," added Roly. So, they sniffed around at the bottom of the fence and then they began to dig. Charlie dug a bit, then Roly dug a bit. Soon, there was a hole just big enough for Charlie to poke his head through.

In next door's garden, there was a trampoline and bouncing up and down on it were Daisy and her friend, Jane. They looked like they were having loads of fun. "Hello," they giggled. "Would you like to play on our trampoline?"
"Yes, please," said Charlie.

When Charlie tried to pull his head out from under the fence, it wouldn't move. "I'm stuck!" he said to Roly. So, Roly pulled and tugged and heaved, but he couldn't get Charlie free. Luckily, Mom was watching from the kitchen window. "I knew you two would get up to mischief," she said, coming outside.

Mom dug and dug and soon, Charlie was free. "Next time, if you need help with something, remember to ask," said Mom, gently. "Sorry," said Charlie. "Sorry," said Roly.
Then they started to fill in the hole.

When the soil was all nice and smooth, Mom took Charlie and Roly next door to play. They had lots of fun, bouncing on the big trampoline with their new friends, Daisy and Jane. Best of all, Mom was there to make sure there was no more mischief.

Heather and the Weather

Heather didn't like the weather. "It keeps changing," she said. On Monday and Tuesday, it was sunny and light, so Heather pulled on her best, red swimsuit and splashed about in the little paddling pool. "I love the sunshine!" she cried.

On Wednesday, clouds pushed in front of the sun and the sky
was moody and grey. "I'll have to wear my jumper and my old
red jeans, now," said Heather. She wasn't happy,
so she scowled and frowned.

On Thursday, the rain fell in blobs and splats. Heather wore
her yellow rain coat and her flowery rain hat, but the rain hat
leaked and Heather got wet. So she ran inside and looked out of
the window. "I don't like the rain," she complained.

On Friday, the sun peeped out. "I can play on the slide," Heather cried. So, Heather put on her best spotty top and her pretty, pink shorts. The sun disappeared and the sky grew dark and very quiet. "I don't like this," said Heather, so she ran inside.

On Saturday, black clouds gathered. "Go away clouds, I want to play," shouted Heather, shaking her fist. The sky rumbled and grumbled. Lightning crackled and flashed. "I don't like storms," said Heather and she shivered and ran inside.

On Sunday, the sun came out and Heather was happy. "You are a bit like the weather," said Mom. "Sometimes you're clouds and rain. Sometimes you're thunder and lightning. Mostly, you're like soft, summer sunshine."

The Big Toy Shop

Elsie's Teddy was very, very old. "I think it's time we let Old Teddy have a rest," said Mom. "Let's go to the toy shop and you can choose a brand new one." So, Elsie and her mom went off to the big toy shop.

Inside the shop, there were lots of teddy bears. Elsie didn't know which one to choose. Then, suddenly, she heard a voice say, "Hello." It was Elsie's friend, Tom, and he had come to look at the teddy bears, too.

"The stuffing has all come out of my teddy," said Tom, showing it to Elsie. "Mommy says I can have a new one. We could look for one together." So, Elsie and Tom went to look at the teddy bears while their moms had a chat.

All the teddies were neatly displayed, but there was one little bear sitting all on his own. He wore a bright blue jacket with red, patterned trousers, a little felt hat and small, furry boots.
"He's lovely," said Elsie.
"He's cute," said Tom.

They looked at their moms and they looked at the little teddy. Then, at the same time, Tom and Elsie both said, "I want this one!" Elsie took one arm and Tom took the other and they both began to pull. "He's mine," said Tom.
"No, he's mine," said Elsie.

They pulled the teddy this way and that.
"I want him!" said Elsie and she pulled at the little teddy's hat.
"No, I want him!" said Tom and he tugged at the teddy's boot.
Then, suddenly, the hat came off and a boot came loose.

Tom toppled backwards and fell on the floor and Elsie landed with a bump, on her bottom. "Ouch!" they both said, looking very surprised. Their moms looked very surprised, too.
"It's not nice to squabble," they said.

Just then, the shop assistant came over holding another teddy,
just like the other one. "Here you are," she said. "Now you can
have a teddy each." Elsie and Tom felt silly for squabbling.
They were glad they had new teddies to cuddle.

Alice's Surprise

Alice and her friends, Pip and Max, were dressing up for Halloween. "I'm going to be a witch," said Pip, pulling on a tall, black hat.

"I'm going to be a wizard," said Alice, waving a sparkly wand.
"I'm going to be a ghost with rattling chains," said Max and
he pulled on a sheet with holes for eyes. Suddenly, there was a
noise on the stairs. It was a chinking, clinking, clanging sort of
noise and it was coming closer.

"What is it?" asked Pip.
"It sounds like chains clanking," replied Alice.
"What if it's a real ghost?" whispered Max.
At the top of the stairs, the strange noise stopped.
Suddenly, there was a bump against the bedroom door.

Alice screamed. Pip screamed. Max screamed, too. Pip dived
under the bed. Alice jumped into the dressing-up box and Max
hid in the wardrobe. Very slowly, the door began to open
and a clinking, clanging shape came in.

Alice stared. Pip stared. Max stared, too. Alice thought the shadow looked very familiar. Then, a big, deep voice boomed, "Where is everyone? I've brought you lemonade and cookies." It was Alice's dad. "We thought you were a ghost," said Alice.

"No," laughed Dad. "It was just the glasses chinking, as I walked
up the stairs. Come on, you lot. I think you need
a drink and a cookie after all that excitement."
So they had lemonade, cookies and a very spooky Halloween.

Nigel's Brush

It was painting day at Nigel's house. Mom put a new sheet of paper on the easel. Nigel got out his paints, his blue dungarees and his big, special brush. "Let's mix some paints," said Mom. "Not too runny and not too thick."

Nigel smiled and picked up his brush. He was just about to dip it into some paint when, *drring, drring,* the telephone rang. "Wait a minute, Nigel," said Mom and she went into the hall.

Nigel didn't want to wait. With a gloop and a splosh he dipped his big, special brush into a pot of pink paint and went SPLODGE, onto the clean, white paper.
"It's fun!" said Nigel, swishing his brush. Then, he cleaned it in a glass of water and dipped it into another pot of paint. Nigel giggled and splashed the bright paints in his paint tray.

Then, *click*, went the phone in the hallway and Mom came
back in. She looked at Nigel and she looked at the picture.
Her eyes grew wide and her mouth grew wider.
"Nigel!" she cried. "I told you to wait. You're covered in paint."

"I drew a picture of you, Mommy," said Nigel, with a smile. Mom sighed and then she smiled, too. "Thank you, Nigel," she said. "That's very kind of you, but I think we need to go upstairs and get you cleaned up."

Mom took Nigel upstairs. "Take off those dirty
dungarees," she said, "and jump into this nice, soapy bath."
"If it rains, can we do painting tomorrow?" asked Nigel.
"Yes," said Mom. "Next time, we'll do it together."

Mom Says, "Goodnight"

Bradley was looking at his new space monster book. "Are there really monsters in space?" he asked Mom. "No, there's no such thing," said Mom, gently. "Come on, it's bedtime. You go upstairs and I'll come and tuck you in."

So, Bradley ran upstairs, brushed his teeth and put on his soft, stripy pajamas. Then, he jumped into bed and waited for Mom to come and tuck him in. Bradley waited and waited, but Mom didn't come.

The wind blew clouds across the moon and rattled
Bradley's window. He looked outside at the shadows and shapes.
"What if space monsters really do exist?" whispered Bradley.
"What if they come from the moon, into my room?"

Just then, Bradley heard a shuffle on the stairs and saw a shadow stretch up over the banister and along the wall. "Is that you, Mom?" whispered Bradley, in a scared voice. No one answered. So, Bradley sunk right down and pulled his quilt up to his chin. "Are you a space monster?" he called out.

"No, Bradley," said a soft, laughing voice. "It's me, Mommy
and I've come to tuck you in, kiss you goodnight
and tell you a story. Not one about space monsters."
Bradley was very relieved. He still loved space monsters, but
he was glad that they only existed in books.

Activity Page

See if you can answer these questions about the stories in 'My First Playtime Story Book'.

1. In 'Playtime Fun', which toy goes *bang*?

2. What game is Amy playing with Daddy in 'Amy's Game'?

3. What animal is the lifeguard in 'Bubbles Learns to Swim'?

4. Who does Walter rescue in 'Walter to the Rescue'?

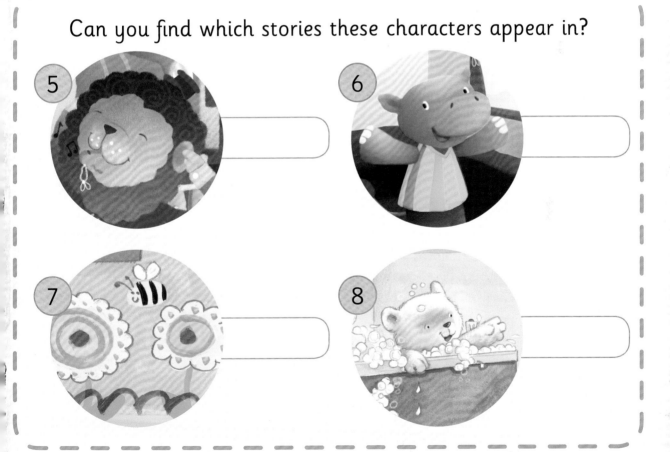

Can you find which stories these characters appear in?

Goodbye and see you soon!